**Put Beginning Readers on the Right Track with
ALL ABOARD READING™**

The All Aboard Reading series is especially designed for beginning readers. Written by noted authors and illustrated in full color, these are books that children really want to read—books to excite their imagination, expand their interests, make them laugh, and support their feelings. With fiction and nonfiction stories that are high interest and curriculum-related, All Aboard Reading books offer something for every young reader. And with four different reading levels, the All Aboard Reading series lets you choose which books are most appropriate for your children and their growing abilities.

**Picture Readers**
Picture Readers have super-simple texts, with many nouns appearing as rebus pictures. At the end of each book are 24 flash cards—on one side is a rebus picture; on the other side is the written-out word.

**Station Stop 1**
Station Stop 1 books are best for children who have just begun to read. Simple words and big type make these early reading experiences more comfortable. Picture clues help children to figure out the words on the page. Lots of repetition throughout the text helps children to predict the next word or phrase—an essential step in developing word recognition.

**Station Stop 2**
Station Stop 2 books are written specifically for children who are reading with help. Short sentences make it easier for early readers to understand what they are reading. Simple plots and simple dialogue help children with reading comprehension.

**Station Stop 3**
Station Stop 3 books are perfect for children who are reading alone. With longer text and harder words, these books appeal to children who have mastered basic reading skills. More complex stories captivate children who are ready for more challenging books.

GROSSET & DUNLAP
Published by the Penguin Group
Penguin Group (USA) Inc., 375 Hudson Street, New York, New York 10014, USA
Penguin Group (Canada), 90 Eglinton Avenue East, Suite 700, Toronto, Ontario M4P 2Y3,
Canada (a division of Pearson Penguin Canada Inc.)
Penguin Books Ltd., 80 Strand, London WC2R 0RL, England
Penguin Group Ireland, 25 St. Stephen's Green, Dublin 2, Ireland (a division of Penguin Books Ltd.)
Penguin Group (Australia), 250 Camberwell Road, Camberwell, Victoria 3124, Australia
(a division of Pearson Australia Group Pty. Ltd.)
Penguin Books India Pvt. Ltd., 11 Community Centre, Panchsheel Park, New Delhi—110 017, India
Penguin Group (NZ), 67 Apollo Drive, Rosedale, North Shore 0632, New Zealand
(a division of Pearson New Zealand Ltd.)
Penguin Books (South Africa) (Pty.) Ltd., 24 Sturdee Avenue,
Rosebank, Johannesburg 2196, South Africa
Penguin Books Ltd., Registered Offices: 80 Strand, London WC2R 0RL, England

*Library of Congress Cataloging-in-Publication Data is available.*

ISBN 978-0-448-45260-9          10 9 8 7 6 5 4 3 2

# ALL ABOARD READING™

**Station Stop 2**

## nickelodeon The PENGUINS of MADAGASCAR™

DREAMWORKS®

## HAPPY KING JULIEN DAY!

by Olivia London

Grosset & Dunlap

An Imprint of Penguin Group (USA) Inc.

Night had fallen in the New York zoo.

But the Zoovenir Shop was full of animals.

Suddenly, King Julien

burst into the room. *Ta-da!*

Mort pressed play on the stereo.

Loud cheering came out of the speakers,

but the animals just stared blankly.

"In a few hours, we celebrate the biggest

holiday of the year!" King Julien said.

"Christmas in July!" Marlene shouted.

Then she thought for a moment.

"Except . . . it's not Christmas,

and it's not July," she realized.

"Look how they tease me," King Julien joked.

"I am speaking of King Julien Day!

It is on every calendar!"

King Julien showed them a calendar

with his face drawn on it.

"So start shopping!" he said.

The animals had no idea

what King Julien was talking about.

"What is King Julien Day?" asked Marlene.

"Everyone gives gifts to the king

and does whatever he says,"

Maurice explained.

"I see," said Skipper. "In that case, pass!"

With that, he turned to leave the room.

The other animals followed Skipper.

But Maurice shouted for them to wait.

"You want King Julien

to be happy on his holiday!" he called.

"You do *not* want him to freak on you!"

"We'll take our chances,"

Skipper replied from the doorway.

"Please!" Mort begged. "King Julien Day

is my favorite holiday. I love it this much!"

Mort stretched his arms wide.

He was cute, but the animals

still weren't sure.

Luckily, Maurice had a plan.

He lifted a piñata in the air.

He had found it at

a birthday party at the zoo.

"Do you know what people

put in these things?" asked Maurice.

"Candy!"

That got the penguins' attention.

Suddenly everyone was thinking

about lollipops and chocolate.

"This piñata is full of delicious sweets,"

Maurice said.

"They can all be yours if you celebrate

King Julien Day like you mean it."

Candy changed everything.

The animals agreed to celebrate

King Julien Day.

Back in the penguin habitat,

Skipper's crew was guessing

what was inside the piñata.

"I bet it's a mix of gummy fish

and candy buttons," Kowalski said.

"We may never know," said Skipper.

"Because tonight we are cleaning."

"Perhaps we could postpone?"
Kowalski asked.

"Negative!" Skipper replied.

Then he crossed King Julien Day

off his calendar.

"Skipper's right," said Private.

"Candy is candy."

He shook his head. "I mean, duty is duty!"

Private, Kowalski, and Rico thought about

all the candy they would not get to eat.

They could not help being sad.

Kowalski even cried a single tear.

Skipper felt bad. "Okay," he said.

"I will clean by myself. You can go!"

The others could not believe their ears.

They would get to eat candy after all!

When King Julien Day arrived,

King Julien was very excited.

"Welcome, my loyal, royal subjects!"

he called to the animals.

"Happy King Julien Day!" Marlene shouted.

Maurice stood where King Julien

could not see him.

He held up the piñata

to remind the animals of their prize.

Then he called out,

"Everyone, now bask in the glory

that is King Julien!"

The animals *ooh*ed and *ahh*ed loudly.

But not loudly enough for the king.

"That was weak!" King Julien cried.

"And you *know* how that

makes me feel, Maurice!"

King Julien was getting angry.

So Maurice tried to change the subject.

"Let's get this party started!" he said.

"Everybody, time to limbo!"

"Yes!" cried King Julien. "Limbo contest!"

So the animals lined up to limbo.

Marlene was the first to go.

Her nose almost touched the pole,

but she made it!

"Must have candy," she whispered,

reminding herself to stick with it.

Just as Rico stepped up to the pole,

King Julien lowered it a few inches.

But Rico coughed up an anchor,

and spit it out.

Then he slipped right under.

Finally, all of the animals

made it under the pole.

Then it was King Julien's turn.

The pole was very low.

None of the animals could limbo

under this pole—except for King Julien.

He leaned back very far,

and walked right under!

"King Julien wins

the limbo contest!"

Maurice announced.

"I am not only *the* king,"

King Julien replied.

"I am the *limbo* king, too!"

"Next, we do the traditional King Julien Day tossing of the fruit!" Maurice said.

"Tossing it where, exactly?" Marlene asked.

Just then, King Julien threw a hard, juicy melon.

He hit Marlene right in the face!

"Julien tosses it at you," Maurice replied.

"At us? No!" said Kowalski.

But then Mort secretly showed

the piñata to the animals.

Soon everyone was thinking about

gumballs and toffee.

They decided to let King Julien

toss the fruit.

King Julien picked up a giant pineapple.

He tossed it at Phil,

knocking him to the ground.

Mason thought that was funny . . .

until he got hit by a giant mango!

Next, King Julien hit Private

in the face with a huge watermelon.

The animals could not wait

for the tossing of the fruit to end.

After putting up with all of this,

they really deserved that candy!

Back at the penguin habitat,

Skipper was hard at work cleaning.

He had just finished wiping the telescope

when a piece of fruit flew through the air.

It splattered right on the lens!

"I just cleaned that!" he cried.

At the party,

all the fruit had been tossed.

"Next is the bake-off!" Maurice said.

"You have one hour to bake the best

King Julien Day cake ever!"

King Julien thought everyone

would rush off to bake.

But the animals just stood there.

"Does anyone know how to bake?"

Marlene asked.

The animals all shook their heads.

"Why are they shaking when they should

be baking?" King Julien asked angrily.

His eyes opened wide and his face got red.

Maurice secretly showed the animals

the piñata.

Once again, the candy did its job!

"I have always wanted to learn baking,"

Private said suddenly.

And the animals ran off to bake.

Kowalski, Private, and Rico went back

to the habitat to bake Julien's cake.

Their first step was finding a mixing spoon.

Luckily, Rico was able to cough one up!

Phil and Mason kept monkeying around.

Phil put pineapples on his eyes.

And Mason smashed the eggs

with a rolling pin!

Marlene had never stirred so much.

She was very tired.

Baking a cake was hard work!

Then Mort came by with the piñata.

The thought of candy woke her up!

Finally it was time to show

the cakes to King Julien.

Marlene went first.

Her cake was made with flies and worms.

"I am on a low-tick diet!"

King Julien said. "Next!"

Mason handed King Julien

their pineapple cake.

"It's frosted with brown booger," he said.

Then Phil used sign language

to say something to Mason.

"My mistake, I mean brown *sugar*."

"Well, just in case . . . Next!" the king said.

Finally, the penguins gave him their cake.

"Death by chocolate," Kowalski said.

King Julien licked his lips.

"The chocolate part sounds good!" he said.

"Actually, we used mud," they told him.

"Bring it here so that my belly

may taste its yumminess!" cried Julien.

"I'll bring it!" said Mort.

Mort grabbed the cake.

But then he tripped.

The cake went flying!

King Julien got mad. Again.

"I was looking forward to

eating my cake!" he yelled.

Skipper had just finished

cleaning fruit off the telescope lens.

Then the flying cake landed on his head!

Skipper marched over to the king.

"News flash!" he shouted.

"There is no such thing as King Julien Day!"

The animals could not believe their ears.

They had worked so hard to keep King Julien

happy so they could get candy.

But now he would get *really* angry!

Maurice lowered his head in his hands.

Mort was so upset, he fainted!

Everyone just stood there, waiting to see

what King Julien would do next.

King Julien's eyes opened very wide.

He leaned in close to Skipper,

who still had the cake on his head.

"My cake!" he cried. "It's back!"

Everyone sighed with relief—

especially Maurice.

King Julien was so happy to see his cake,

he had not heard what Skipper said!

"Silly penguin," King Julien said,

taking the cake off Skipper's head.

"Have some cake *in* your head, not on it!

Why, I think this was the best

King Julien Day ever!"

Then Julien went off to eat his cake.

"You saved my big old behind, Skipper!"

Maurice said.

"And you helped this crew win one big piñata!"

"Candy! Candy!" they all cheered.

They were finally going to eat the

gummy fish and candy buttons!

But just as they were about to break

it open, King Julien came back.

"What is this? You got me a

big paper horse?" he asked.

"Thank you! I will name him Bob."

"Um, your majesty, that's actually a piñata,"

Maurice explained.

He thought the animals deserved their candy.

But King Julien just laughed. "A pin-whata?

Why are you making up words, Maurice?"

Then he hopped on Bob and bounced away.

46

But King Julien bounced right back.
"Silly king me, I almost forgot
the traditional King Julien Day
sharing of the sweets!" he said.

"Bob has candy guts," King Julien cried.

"So dig in!"

Then he tore a giant hole in the piñata.

Candy spilled out of Bob.

At last, everyone enjoyed

the sweet, yummy treats!

It *was* the best King Julien Day ever!